This is Hot Wheels City!
The city is made for car lovers.
There are racetracks everywhere!

This is the Hot Wheels Ultimate Garage.
Every car gets made here!

Dash Wheeler is a great racer.
She started the Ultimate Garage.

Dash has invited six kids to the Ultimate Garage Racing Camp. They all love racing!

They will learn a lot.
They all want to be Hot Wheels City's best racers one day.

Coop is a Hot Wheels
super fan who has a
need for speed.
He works very hard
and always wants to
do better.
He wants to be
Camp Champ.

Spark is very smart.
She loves to learn
and come up with
new ideas.
She keeps trying if
they do not work.

Mac loves to take risks.
He likes stunts and
anything fast.
He is always having fun.

Axle's dad is the best
racer driving today.
Axle thinks he is the
best too.
He is very good but
everyone can get better.

Sidecar is Axle's
best friend.
He loves to help
Axle win.

Brights likes to do things her own way. This can help with her driving.

Squeakers is a robot
who runs Dash's lab.
He has lots of tools.
He helps the campers
fix their cars.

Professor Rearview is the one person in Hot Wheels City who does not like driving.
He wants to stop all the cars.

Each Hot Wheels car is special.

Baja Jump Truck can do a big jump.

This car is *Rodger Dodger.*
It is great to drive.
It can take very fast corners.

This is the *Carbonator.*
It looks like a big bottle.
It can blast water.

This car is called the *Roller Toaster*.
It can shoot toast out of its roof!

The GT *Scorcher* is really fast.
It has a super speed burst.
It goes so fast that flames come off
the tyres.

The *Donut Drifter* looks like a big donut!
It can do a sweet spin.